GHOST
WRITER

GHOST WRITER

Edgar J. Hyde

CCP

© 1998 Children's Choice Publications

Text supplied by Simon Bedding

All rights reserved. No part of this publication may be reproduced, stored in a retrieval systemor transmitted, in any form or by any means, electronic, mechanical, photocopying, recording, or otherwise without the prior consent of the copyright holder.

ISBN 1-90201-206-2

Printed and bound in the UK

CONTENTS

Chapter 1

It was late Saturday afternoon and verging upon evening. Charlie, Neil, and Kate were all packing to get ready for moving house. They had been busy clearing up the last few bits and pieces in their drawers and cupboards before the final removal van took the last of their possessions to the "new" house.

Charlie was the eldest and was 15 years of age. His blonde hair was parted down the centre and he had a rugged look about him. Neil was 13 and was of average height. He had dark brown eyes and shortly cropped brown hair. Their sister, Kate, was about the same height with medium-long blonde hair and dark, mysterious eyes. She was 14 years old.

The teenagers were moving to a bigger, older

house with a huge garden on the other side of town.

"Oh no! No!" cried Neil, from his bedroom.

Charlie and Kate rushed into his room.

"What's up?" asked Charlie.

"I can't find the games for the Nintendo!" answered Neil.

"They've been packed already remember?" said Kate, "You put them in a box outside your door.

"Oh yeah," remembered Neil in relief.

"You dope!" said Charlie, "I would've killed you if you'd lost them - they cost absolute loads."

"You'd better get your stuff packed quickly Neil - Dad wants us down and ready to go in five minutes," said Kate.

"Come on!" called Dad suddenly, from downstairs. "Get your stuff together, we're off!"

"Coming!" called Neil.

"Yeah, coming!" called Charlie and Kate together.

Charlie took one more look at his now empty bedroom before picking up the last box of his possessions walking downstairs.

"Come on Charlie," called Neil who was already in the car with Kate, "we're going!"

Chapter 1

"Coming," replied Charlie, quickly lobbing his box haphazardly into the back of the removal van. He then leapt into the back of the car.

Neil was sitting in the middle of the car and Kate was on the left. Mum was on the passenger seat and Dad was in the driver's seat.

As soon as Charlie was in, Dad started the engine and drove off.

They arrived at the house at half past eight and, as it was late Autumn, it was pitch black. The house was on the other side of town and was much bigger than the one they had just left. It was also much older. The walls were whitewashed but seriously in need of repair. The windows were tall with pointed arches and reflected the glare of the cars headlights as it turned into the drive. Dad had been doing the more important repair jobs in the past two months but the house was still in need of considerable renovation.

The teenagers clambered out of the back of the car and followed their parents up the path to the front door. Dad spent a while turning the key in the lock.

"I haven't got round to oiling it yet," was his explanation.

They all walked into the porch and Charlie shut the door behind him. He had to push it closed with some force as it didn't swing at all.

Dad fumbled for the light switch. Upon finding it he flicked it. The lights came on for a few seconds until they flickered and then died out.

"Damn!" exclaimed Dad, "I'll have to sort out the fuse box - Charlie get the torch from the car."

"Okay Dad," replied Charlie.

Charlie took the keys from his dad and opened the front door again. He walked down the path until he reached the car. He put the key in the lock and turned it. Upon hearing the sound of the motors of the central locking whirring he opened the rear-left door and took the torch from the map pocket at the back of the front seat.

He tested it quickly by flashing it on and then off. Then he locked the car and hurried back inside.

When he had closed the front door behind him he found only his Dad waiting there.

"Where are the others?" asked Charlie as he handed the keys back to his father.

"They've gone through to the kitchen," replied Dad. "You might as well join them and help get some food made - I'll sort out the fuse box by myself."

"Okay," answered Charlie.

In the kitchen he found the gas cooker on - giving the room a bit of light - and Neil trying to get a fire going in the ancient fire place. Kate and Mum were sitting opposite each other, talking quietly, at the old kitchen table which had come with the house. Charlie sat down next to Mum and idly watched Neil trying to get the fire alight.

"You're not going to be able to do it," taunted Charlie.

"How much you gonna bet on that then?" replied Neil arrogantly.

"I think a fiver will do nicely - I bet that you won't get the fire going before the electricity's back on," replied Charlie.

"You're on," answered Neil.

Over the next ten minutes Charlie watched as Neil tried to get the fire alight.

Suddenly, with no warning, a light flickered in the hallway from the direction of the porch. The light dimmed, then steadied itself out and remained constant.

"A fiver please Neil," said Charlie smugly.

"Fine - that's the last time I ever bet with you," replied Neil, handing the five pound note over to Charlie.

"We're even now - remember yesterday I lost that bet to you," said Charlie.

"You shouldn't keep betting you two," said Kate suddenly. "You're just going to lose all your money."

"Or win it," grinned Charlie.

Neil laughed.

"Perhaps she's got a point though Charlie - I do always lose."

"Then don't bet," answered Charlie as Dad entered.

"Alright then people, do you want food or do you just want to go to bed?" he asked.

"Food!" replied the teenagers.

After a quick meal they went to their chosen rooms and fell into their beds which had been put there the day before. They were all asleep almost as soon as their heads touched their pillows.

Chapter 2

The next morning Charlie was the first to wake up. He got washed and dressed, then looked at his watch.

It was half past eight and there was nothing to do so he decided to start work on his latest short story for the local youth club's weekly magazine. He enjoyed doing this and wrote a new story for each issue. The stories took up only a page in the magazine but Charlie hoped to write a whole novel one day. At the moment he was doing a serial so he was writing the short story now for several issues ahead.

He sat down with his pen and pad and thought for a while. Then he began writing.

At half past nine Neil peered into his room and said:

"Morning Charlie. It's time for breakfast - Dad's just cooked us a fry-up."

"OK," replied Charlie, "I'll be down in a second."

Charlie looked down at his pad for a second and then finished off the sentence he was working on. He placed his biro neatly next to the pad and stood up.

Down in the kitchen, Dad was just serving up eggs, bacon, sausages and mushrooms onto the plates laid out around the old, worn, kitchen table.

He looked up as Neil entered, followed shortly afterwards by Charlie.

"Morning Charlie!" greeted Dad cheerfully, "Have a good sleep?"

"Yeah," replied Charlie, "and you?"

"Fine thanks," answered Dad, sitting down at his place next to Mum, "Where's Kate?"

"She's coming down any minute," said Neil, whilst also sitting down, "What are we doing today?"

"Well, as it's the first day of your week's holiday I thought you might like to give us a hand unpacking," said Dad.

Chapter 2

"Great," said Kate unenthusiastically as she entered the kitchen.

"You sound cheerful Kate," said Charlie.

"Great," repeated Kate more enthusiastically as she saw the contents of the kitchen table, "a fried breakfast - just what I need."

"I thought that might cheer you up," said Dad, smiling, "and I'm glad you eventually decided to join us," he continued with a trace of sarcasm.

Kate grinned and sat down at the empty space left for her at the table.

For a few minutes, there was complete silence, except for the sound of five hungry people tucking into breakfast. Eventually Dad sat back, wiped his face with some kitchen roll and sighed.

"I really needed that," he said with a contented smile.

"You look like you somehow enjoyed that," said Mum.

"You're right, I did," replied Dad.

The teenagers cleared up the table and washed up whilst Mum and Dad got washed and dressed for the day.

By eleven o'clock, everyone was ready to start unpacking all the things they had brought from their old house.

The furniture had been unpacked a few days previously and had been laid out in the correct places already. All the family had to do was unpack their personal possessions such as clothes and ornaments.

The teenagers began to unpack their own possessions and put them away in cupboards and drawers. By six o'clock they had almost finished personalising their bedrooms. They decided to call it a day and finish the remainder of their unpacking the next day.

After dinner, Neil and Kate played against each other on their games console whilst Charlie tried to finish his short story. By nine thirty the teenagers decided to go to bed and have an early night.

Charlie set his pen and pad next to his bed and read the last few words to himself:

James knelt down and tried to prise the lid off of the box but it was stuck.

As he lay in bed he wondered how he could continue the plot. He was still mulling over it as he fell sound asleep.

Chapter 3

"Wake up Charlie."

Charlie sat up and rubbed his eyes.

"Wha'?" he asked, still half asleep.

"I said: wake up Charlie," said Neil, standing in the doorway, "It's nine o'clock."

"OK," replied Charlie shaking his head and wondering why he hadn't woken up earlier. It wasn't like him to sleep for twelve hours. He glanced at his bedside clock and to see if it really was nine o'clock. As his gaze swept across his bedside table he happened to glance at his pad. Without quite knowing why, he picked the pad up and read the last few words on it:

Suddenly, The lid flew open and James' hand slipped. His hand caught on one of the nails sticking from the side of the box.

He clutched his hand as blood began to seep through a gash in his index finger.

Charlie sat there for a few seconds, taken aback by the words that he could not remember adding to the end of his story the night before. He shrugged thinking that he must have woken up and written it in the night. Perhaps that was why he had woken up so late this morning?

Charlie put the pad back on table and got up. What he had failed to notice was that although he had written the story in biro yesterday, the new sentence, whilst written in his own handwriting, was in fountain pen ink.

Breakfast was not as elaborate as the day before. Charlie had cornflakes with a glass of orange juice. After breakfast he unpacked and sorted his possessions, before helping his parents to pack all of the kitchen items into their correct places.

By half past four Charlie and his parents had finished organising the kitchen and were ready to tackle tidying the rest of the house. Neil and Kate helped out with this and by eight o'clock they were halfway through the job. After a very constructive day working together, the family decided to finish work for the day and Mum and

Chapter 3

Dad began to make the dinner. Charlie, Neil and Kate had a game of cards in the large dining room. The dining room was dimly lit with a large round table in the middle. The children where sitting on one side of the table.

"I win!" exclaimed Neil. "Again!"

"Damn - how do you do it?" asked Charlie, tossing a couple of pennies over to Neil.

"He cheats probably," said Kate, also throwing a few coins in Neil's direction.

"How about another game?" asked Neil, ignoring Kate's remark. "Shall we up the stakes a little? I'll raise you five pence."

"OOh – big money! Okay," said Charlie throwing a few pennies into the middle of the table.

"Five pence it is," said Kate doing the same. The teenagers continued their game until about nine o'clock. By this time Charlie decided that he had lost quite enough money to Neil and wanted to add more to his short story He left Neil and Kate playing cards and went up to his room. Feeling a bit lonely upstairs, he decided to return to the dining room and write at the window seat there.

In the dining room the tables had turned and Kate had just won ten pence back from Neil.

The teenagers didn't bet large amounts of money because they only played cards for fun.

Charlie sat down at the window seat, against the black background of the night outside, and thought for a while, whilst sucking his pen. Then he began writing

For one hour he wrote until, at ten o'clock, he was half way through the second part of the series.

Neil and Kate were packing up the cards and Charlie flipped the latest page on his pad over to reveal a new sheet of paper. He took the pad upstairs and lay it on his bedside table again before having a bath and getting into bed.

For half an hour he read a book, until at a quarter to eleven he tossed the book onto the pad and switched off his bedside light. Within minutes he was asleep.

*   *   *

Suddenly Charlie awoke with a start. He was in a room - he felt trapped. The door to the room was almost fully bricked up. A face glanced into the room and láughed before placing another brick onto the wall blocking up the door. Soon the last brick went in and the last shaft of flickering light - perhaps candle light - disappeared and he was alone in the dark. He started calling for help, but his voice was muffled by the walls. He called again and again. He began to panic as his heart beat faster and faster. He stood up and staggered forward. He hit a wall and rebounded off it. He became disorientated as he staggered around the room - he lost track of up and down. He hit a corner and staggered backwards. He found another wall and started to beat against the stone, then he began to scrabble and try to dig his way through with his finger nails whilst screaming to be let out. Charlie began to become dizzy as the air in the room grew stale and the oxygen ran out. He was slowly beginning to suffocate. Charlie stepped back and stopped screaming before suddenly collapsing to the floor as he passed out. He barely felt hitting the ground. Before Charlie completely lost consciousness he heard demonic laughter echoing into the distance. Then his body went limp and Charlie lay unconscious on the floor as he slowly suffocated to death.

*   *   *

Charlie sat up with a start. The weak autumn sun was shining through the window and he was in bed. He was drenched in a cold sweat and the bed sheets were tightly entwined around his body. He relaxed and sighed - it was only a dream.

Charlie remembered the dream and shuddered - it had seemed so real - and scary. The feeling of the claustrophobia he had felt in the dream came back briefly. It soon subsided and Charlie began wondering what to do that day.

The dream completely forgotten, Charlie got up and had a shower. He dressed and picked up his watch from his bedside table next to the pad with half a page of his neat writing on it. Charlie then went downstairs and made himself a quick breakfast before going into the lounge to watch morning television. He found Neil in there, sitting on the floor watching television

"Morning Neil," greeted Charlie.

"Morning," replied Neil chewing his thumb nail.

"What's on telly?" asked Charlie

"Just the usual rubbish," said Neil. Neil stood up and settled himself onto the settee before sticking his thumb back into his mouth.

They watched breakfast television for half an hour before Mum came down and asked Charlie and Neil to get some groceries from the nearby local shop.

Chapter 3

They set off along the worn road, strolling at a leisurely pace.

"How's the story going?" asked Neil casually as the boys walked side-by-side down the street.

"Fine," said Charlie vacantly, as the boys stood on the grass verge to let a car go by. Neil looked at Charlie's face and saw that he wasn't really concentrating on what Neil was saying and instead was thinking.

"What are you thinking about?" asked Neil.

"Oh nothing - just a dream," replied Charlie shaking his head as if to remove the memories of the dream.

Five minutes later they reached the shop and went in. It was unfamiliar to them as previously they had lived on the other side of town and subsequently hardly came to this area.

The shop was quite old fashioned. Instead of the bright fluorescent lights found in most modern shops, there was a solitary bulb hanging from the ceiling. The shelves were stacked with tins of food, made by little-known manufacturers. All of the shelves had a thick layer of dust, indicating not just that no-one cleaned the place very often, but that they didn't seem to have much success at selling anything either.

At the counter, which was next to the door, there was a till and a couple of charity boxes. There was no-one at the till, but behind the string curtain there was a sound of a whistling. Charlie picked up a rusting basket distastefully and the boys began putting the items from the list into it. They had nearly finished when suddenly there was a triumphant cry from the counter.

"Hah! I told 'em! I told 'em! But would they listen? Would they ever! I've caught you at it you young ruffians, stealing from me - I've got you this time!" An old man had come from behind the curtain and was pointing a shaking finger at the boys.

"Actually we're buying this stuff," said Charlie, gesturing with his wallet. "Unlikely as it may seem," he muttered under his breath, looking at a suspiciously rusty tin of spam.

"Yah, okay," said the old man settling back into a chair behind the counter.

Charlie and Neil hurriedly finished finding the last items on the list and then went to the counter. The old man worked out the cost and charged Charlie accordingly. The man hit the lever on the old fashioned till and scraped out the change for the boys.

Chapter 3

"I ain't seen ya 'ere before," said the old man. "You new?"

"We moved from the other side of town," replied Neil.

"I take that as a 'yes'," grumbled the old man, "Where ya moved to - somewhere nearby?"

"Into the empty house in Two Oaks Road," said Neil before Charlie could stop him.

"Haaa-haaaaa-haaaaa!" laughed the old man suddenly, "You've moved into the 'aunted 'ouse!"

"'Aunted 'ouse?" asked Charlie, "What do you mean?"

"I mean what I say," grinned the man. "That 'ouse is 'aunted."

"Oh! Haunted house," said Charlie smiling. "You mean haunted house."

"Yeah, that's right - 'aunted 'ouse."

"That's alright I don't believe in ghosts," said Charlie.

"That's what they all say," said the old man with a sinister smile, "before it 'appens."

"Before what 'appens - I mean happens?" demanded Neil.

"You'll see sonny," replied the old man, "You'll see."

With that, the old man turned abruptly and went back through the bead curtain laughing.

"Before what happens?" asked Neil again, half to himself.

"Nothing - he's just trying to scare us, that's all," said Charlie, as he led the way out of the shop, "The bloke must get kicks out of scaring local kids."

"Mean spirited old so and so," spat Neil.

"He probably gets bored working in that smelly shop," said Charlie, trying to be fair.

"Yeah, it did pong a bit," answered Neil as they began to walk up the hill towards the house.

The boys entered the house at half past nine. By this time everyone was up and about. Kate had just finished breakfast and was watching television. She looked up as Charlie and Neil entered the lounge having just deposited the shopping in the kitchen.

"Hi," she greeted.

"Hi Kate," replied Charlie.

"Yeah hi," said Neil.

"What shall we do today?" asked Kate.

"How about searching the attic for any old stuff left here from the people before," suggested Charlie.

Chapter 3

"Okay," agreed Kate.

"Alright," said Neil.

The teenagers were up in the attic in almost no time at all. It was basically empty except for three old boxes in one corner. Charlie opened the first box. It was wooden, and after he had removed the lid revealed nothing but a small pile of old sawdust. Charlie moved over to the next one and lifted the lid. The result was the same - just a small pile of sawdust.

Disheartened Charlie began to lift the lid of the last and smallest box. The lid shifted and then stuck. Charlie tugged the lid again but the lid still refused to move. Charlie changed his grip on it and tried again. Suddenly the lid shot open and Charlie staggered back.

"Ow!" he cried as blood began to seep through a deep gash in his left hand. Charlie looked down at the box and saw that he must have caught his hand on a nail protruding from the side. He put his hand into his mouth and sucked it.

"Are you okay?" asked Kate.

"I'm fine - what's in the box?"

"Nothing - no there is something - a book," She bent over and picked the box up from where it had been half concealed by bits of sawdust.

"What's in it?" asked Neil.

"Nothing, it's a diary but there are no entries - no there is one, here on the 15th November."

"That's today," interrupted Neil.

"It says," continued Kate, glancing up at Neil, "'Charles, help me, I need help!'"

"Is that it?" asked Charlie taking the book from Kate.

"Yeah," replied Kate, "What a coincidence that it happened to be today's date.

"And it says 'Charles' in it," said Neil.

"I wonder why he needed help?" said Charlie vacantly.

"Why 'he'?" demanded Kate.

"Or she even," continued Charlie as if he hadn't heard Kate.

"If that's all that's up here shall we go down now?" asked Neil.

"Okay then," answered Charlie, "There's nothing else up here of interest."

The teenagers went down the ladder one by one, before returning the ladder to the garage.

Then Charlie, Kate and Neil didn't do much for the rest of the day - they just messed about, played on the games console and played cards. By the evening Charlie couldn't be bothered to write so he just read the story through from the beginning to check for mistakes. He was sitting in the dining room with Neil and Kate. He read a piece of the story which he wasn't sure about. He stood up from the window seat and went over to Kate to ask her opinion. After she had given him her opinion, Charlie sat down next to her instead of returning to his place on the window seat. He continued reading, occasionally turning a page. He stopped reading for a moment to think for a bit. He half-listened to Neil and Kate playing cards, and looked around the dining room - at the old antique bookcases, which had been in the house when they had arrived, the old sideboard that they had brought from their previous house and the window seat with a depression in middle of the padded fabric, which had occurred from many years of use.

He went back to reading his story again and flipped the page.

Charlie frowned and flipped the page back again. He rubbed the page between his fingers to see if he'd turned two pages.

Charlie shrugged and continued reading the page:

He sat back and took in his surroundings - the bookcases, the sideboard, the window seat.

The two other figures were hunched over the ta-

ble, playing cards. One cried out triumphantly and pulled his winnings towards him.

He then glanced back at the window seat. A shadowy figure was sitting there, quietly smiling to himself.

The person had been there longer than anyone could remember and he always sat at the window smiling to himself.

Suddenly Charlie's eyes glazed over and he reeled back from the pad. He hadn't written this – it was in his writing, yes, but it wasn't written in biro.

Charlie slowly glanced up at the window.

A shadowy figure half raised its hand in acknowledgement. Charlie could just make out a smile beneath the dark shadow of the flat cap the figure wore.

"Neil, Kate!" began Charlie, his voice quivering.

"What Charlie?" asked Kate. She looked in the direction of Charlie's frightened gaze and frowned, "What - did you see something outside?"

Charlie blinked and saw only the window and the seat:

"G-g-g-gho—" stammered Charlie.

"Go where?" asked Kate nervously looking back to the window again. "What is it? Whatever was there isn't there now Charlie."

Charlie shook his head as if trying to clear a thought.

"What's up Charlie? You look like you've seen a ghost," said Neil.

"I think I just have," said Charlie in a suddenly calm voice.

Chapter 4

Charlie showed Neil and Kate the pad with the new writing on it:

"I finished at the bottom of the last page," said Charlie, "but look - suddenly there's this extra writing saying exactly what I was doing in the dining room. Come to think of it, I noticed that extra writing this morning but I didn't really think about it until now."

"Yeah right Charlie, I really believe you," sneered Neil.

"It's true!" maintained Charlie.

"You could have written it in the dining room Charlie," said Kate doubtfully, "There's no such thing as ghosts - you've got us all scared but you're taking this prank a bit far."

"It's not a prank!" insisted Charlie.

"Yeah right, Charlie," said Neil in a patronising voice guaranteed to start a brotherly fight.

"Why can't you believe me?!" pleaded Charlie miserably.

"Because it all sounds a bit unlikely," said Kate kindly. "Now I think we should just forget it - you were probably just imagining things," She threw a warning look across the table to Neil who was just about to say something else. He took the hint and decided to stay tight-lipped.

"What about the story then?" demanded Charlie.

"You probably did it earlier on and forgot about it," replied Kate sensibly.

Charlie relented, "Yeah, that's probably it," he sighed.

"Hi kids!" cried Dad suddenly coming into the room making the three children jump. Dad tossed three bars of chocolate onto the table.

"TV grub - we've got a video out," he explained.

As they exited the room to go to the lounge Charlie - who was the last out - looked back towards the window. A shadowy figure waved at him from the window seat and winked. Charlie hurried out and slammed the door be-

Chapter 4

hind him. Once on the other side of the door he shivered, then quickly followed the rest of the family into the lounge to watch the film. It was *Poltergeist ll.* Charlie wasn't at all surprised.

After what had happened in the last few minutes, Charlie didn't find the film the least bit scary. After the film he thought about the shadowy figure on the window seat and decided to himself that he must have imagined it. Then he asked himself how the extra writing had appeared on his pad.

Having rekindled the fear he had had earlier, he was reluctant to go to bed. As it was the holidays and Mum and Dad didn't mind what time he went to bed, he asked Neil and Kate if they wanted to play cards or a board game - Monopoly perhaps?

Neil and Kate guessed the reason why he wanted to stay up but they didn't say anything, partly because Charlie and the film had unnerved them enough to want to return to a sense of normality.

Neil was the best at Monopoly and always won. No-one had ever beaten him at it ever since he had started playing. Charlie and Kate always tried to gang up on him when they played but to no avail. Charlie was only glad that they didn't play with real money. Neil though, was not.

"I want to be the ship," said Neil, picking up the miniature boat with which he always played.

"Okay, I'll be the car," said Charlie.

"And I'll be the boot," said Kate.

"I wonder why there's a boat in it?" speculated Neil light-heartedly.

"And a dog," continued Charlie.

"I suppose it's my turn to say 'and why is there a hat?'," said Kate wearily.

"That's right," said Neil smiling.

"Shall we start to play?" asked Charlie, "Remember who to pick on Kate, if you want to have a chance of winning."

"Neil?" she replied with an innocent smile.

"That's right," said Charlie grinning and rolling the dice.

After an hour of intense Monopoly playing, Neil emerged victorious. Charlie and Kate weren't at all surprised. The teenagers were in much higher spirits now and happily went to bed having forgotten what had happened earlier on. Charlie wearily set his pad on his bedside table out of habit and slid beneath the cool covers.

Chapter 4

*   *   *

Charlie awoke. He was in the room again, only this time the doorway was only half bricked up. The same face looked over the bricks and laughed at Charlie lying on the floor. The face was easier to distinguish this time - Charlie could make out a beard now among the darkened features. Charlie tried to stand up and escape but he couldn't will his body to move. He felt as if he had been drugged. The face looked at Charlie again and grinned:

"So you're awake now, you dirty piece of slime," the owner of the face said suddenly, looking at Charlie, "This'll teach yer."

Charlie tried to stand up again, this time gaining some movement. He began writhing on the floor, but that was the most he could do. He accidentally hit his head against the rough stone floor and became unconscious.

Suddenly Charlie awoke with a start. He was still in the room. The door to the room was almost fully bricked up - Charlie could see the cement oozing between the bricks. The face glanced into the room again and laughed satanically, before placing another brick onto the wall blocking up the doorway. Soon the last brick went in and the last shaft of flickering light

- probably candle or lamp light - disappeared and he was alone in the dark. He started calling for help, but his voice was muffled by the stone walls. He called again and again. He began to panic as his heart beat faster and faster. He stood up and staggered forward. He hit a wall and rebounded off it. He became disorientated as he staggered around the room - he felt as though he were falling. He hit a corner and staggered backwards. He found another wall and started to beat against the stone, crying for help. Then he began to scrabble and try to dig his way through with his fingernails while screaming to be let out. Charlie began to become dizzy as the air in the room grew stale and the oxygen ran out. He was slowly beginning to suffocate. Charlie stepped back and stopped screaming before suddenly collapsing to the floor as he passed out. He barely felt the hard, stone floor. Before Charlie completely lost consciousness he heard demonic laughter echoing into the distance. Then his body went limp and Charlie lay unconscious on the floor as he slowly suffocated to death.

*   *   *

Chapter 5

The bright morning light sparkled through Charlie's window and Charlie turned over to try to shield his eyes from it. As he awoke he remembered the dream. This time there had been more - only a little, but still more. This morning the sheets had again become knotted around his body, as if he had been moving in his sleep. The sheets were wet from Charlie's sweat.

Charlie felt a chill run down his spine and hoped that he wouldn't dream the dream again tonight. With a conscious effort not to look at his writing pad, Charlie got up and dressed. He remembered the night before and shuddered. That guy in the shop yesterday was right, he thought, this house is haunted.

Charlie went into the bathroom wearily and got washed. He rubbed his eyes and looked at himself in the mirror blearily. There were heavy bags under his eyes, indicating lack of sleep. He decided to have an early night tonight.

Charlie slowly got dressed and went downstairs to the kitchen where Kate was just finishing her cereal.

"My God, Charlie, you look awful," she remarked.

"I feel it - how come you're not tired?" Charlie asked.

"Because we didn't go to bed that late last night," replied Kate.

Charlie thought back for a few seconds and frowned.

"You're right - I didn't go to bed that late, so why am I tired?"

"Search me," answered Kate shrugging, "perhaps you ought to get back to sleep?"

"No, I'm too —yawn— awake now," said Charlie.

"You certainly don't look it," commented Kate.

"Hi people!" greeted Neil cheerfully, before looking at Charlie's face and saying: "You look terrible."

"Cheers," said Charlie in a deadpan voice, "good morning yourself."

"What were you up to last night?" asked Neil.

"Nothing," said Charlie.

"Are you sure?" Neil asked.

"Well," began Charlie, "there was one thing that happened."

"Which was?" urged Neil.

"Well I had this dream yesterday night which I had again last night. The funny thing was that last night the dream was a bit longer - there was more at the beginning."

"What happened in the dream?" quizzed Neil.

"Give me a few minutes and I'll tell you," said Charlie, settling down at the kitchen table and resting his hands on its mottled surface.

Charlie told his brother and sister about the dream. About the dark room. About the bricked up doorway. About the bearded face. About the feeling of claustrophobia. About passing out and waking up with his bed sheets screwed up around his body and covered in his sweat.

"Have you ever dreamed this before?" asked Kate.

"No, I haven't," replied Charlie. "Only since moving here."

Suddenly a look of revelation slid across Neil's face.

"Did the bearded fella' look anything like the shadowy guy last night on the window seat?" he asked Charlie rapidly.

Charlie thought about this for a second and then shook his head.

"No, from what I saw, the shadowy bloke on the window seat didn't have a beard," he answered.

"I wonder why you only began dreaming this dream when we arrived here?" asked Kate.

"I don't know," said Charlie, "But if I dream it tonight then dreaming the same thing twice was no coincidence ."

The teenagers were quiet for a while until Charlie said:

"You know last night when I saw the figure of a man at the window seat?"

"Yes," answered Neil.

"Well when we went into the lounge I was the last one out and saw the figure again - it waved to me."

"Suddenly I really don't feel like believing you again," said Neil.

Chapter 5

"There's more," said Charlie. "Every morning since we arrived here, there has been extra writing on my writing pad which I never wrote. Now unless one of you is playing a practical joke on me, I don't know how it got there."

"Can I see your pad?" asked Kate.

"Sure," said Charlie standing up, "I'll just go and get it."

When Charlie returned he placed the pad onto the table at the latest page.

"Look - more writing," he pointed out, "And it's in different ink - that water based stuff, not biro."

"What does it say?" asked Neil looking at the pad, "Oh, I see, you're right, the ink is different - just about here is where it starts."

Charlie read the new words out loud:

" *'The man awoke and stretched. He had fallen asleep on the window seat again whilst writing his latest book. Suddenly the man recollected what he had to do and sighed. For many years he had been good friends with the person he was about to report to the local policeman. They had gone to school together. But what his friend had done was too terrible to ignore - too terrible.'* "

"Are you sure you didn't write this?" asked Kate.

"Look - I'd know if I wrote something or not wouldn't I?" said Charlie defensively, "I don't know who's doing this but I want it to stop, okay?"

"Okay," answered Kate. "So what should we do?"

"Go into the dining room and watch the bloke in the book wake up," he sighed.

The children went into the dining room apprehensively, to see if the writing was going to become a reality. Neil and Kate still didn't quite believe Charlie but, for some reason, the way he was acting about the whole affair unnerved them and they were beginning to get sucked into a situation they weren't sure they'd be able to get out of.

Charlie flung the door open as he entered the room to fight back his rear. The door hit the wall, bounced back and rebounded off Charlie's shoe.

He barely noticed the door hitting his shoe, as he looked across the room towards the large bay window. On the window seat in front of the window, in the shadow of an almighty oak, which clawed the sky as if it was trying to pull itself higher, was the shadowy figure that Charlie had seen the night before. The figure wore a flat cap and the teenagers could just about make out the criss-cross pattern on the figure's tweed jacket. The figure - a man - sat on the seat with his back resting against the side of the bay window. His head was slumped forward against his knees which were hunched up against his body. The man was obviously slumbering.

Then teenagers could not make out the man's face, as it was hidden half by his flat cap and half by his knees. Suddenly the man began to move. He grunted slightly and sat back, whilst looking out of the window simultaneously, thus shielding his face. The teenagers could make out grey-streaked, greasy, brown hair sticking out at crazy angles from beneath the man's hat. The teenagers could also smell a faint hint of boiled cabbage.

Charlie seemed to pull himself together and stepped forward.

"Who are you? What do you want?" he demanded in sudden anger.

The man ignored him.

"Charlie!" shouted Mum from upstairs suddenly, "What are you shouting about?"

Kate and Neil briefly turned and looked in the direction of Mum's voice.

"Nothing Mum!" Charlie called back also turning around slightly.

"Okay - I'll be down soon okay?"

"Okay Mum!" Charlie replied.

He turned back at the same moment as Kate and Neil and staggered back in shock. The man had gone. Charlie rushed over to the window seat in astonishment and stood there speechless for a few seconds, looking around for the man, but he had gone.

And all that was left was a faint smell of boiled cabbage.

"Where is he?" Charlie almost wailed.

He was sitting with his brother and sister at the dining room table, whilst still looking in the direction of the window seat.

"He can't have just vanished." said Neil unhelpfully.

"Well he has," said Kate, her voice quivering slightly. "But what I want to know is how did he get there?"

"Well at least him being there proved I'm not a liar," said Charlie triumphantly, having snapped out of the trance he had been in when the man had vanished.

"You might be right about a man being there but it could be possible that this guy broke in, fiddled with your pad and then waited until we read it and came in to the dining room," Kate said in a matter-of-fact voice.

"Come on now, Kate, you don't actually believe that now do you? You think he quietly opened the bay window (which actually doesn't open) sneaked upstairs, wrote some stuff on my pad (with a fountain pen he just happened to bring along with him) in exactly the same handwriting as my own, then sneaked downstairs into the dining room until morning (in the hope that nobody would go in there until after they had read my pad), and then waited for a chance to leap out of the window (which still doesn't open) and still very quietly close it again when we all just happened to look away! I'm glad you've got all the sane ideas Kate!"

Kate couldn't say anything for a second or two after Charlie's sudden outburst, but she defended herself weakly by demanding:

"Well what do you think happened then?!"

She instantly regretted saying that as Charlie got even more furious.

"I don't know! But I am going to find out!" he replied, emphasising each verb he spoke. Kate stayed quiet then, as she knew she couldn't say anything else to improve the situation. She was shocked at Charlie's outburst - he was normally a well-balanced person who stayed calm all the time and rarely got annoyed. In the rare occasions he did get annoyed he was never this bad and he always cracked up laughing afterwards because his easygoing nature meant that he could never say something seriously and with emotion for any length of time.

"Something really must be getting to him," she thought. "But what? It must be this house - I'm getting to hate it more and more as these freaky things keep happening."

Chapter 6

The teenagers spent the day doing things by themselves. They didn't really feel like talking to each other after the recent events. Charlie stayed in his bedroom at his desk, thinking and occasionally scribbling things down on a scrap of paper. Kate read a book in her room and Neil read a magazine in the lounge. Mum and Dad had gone out to an antiques fair in the next town and wouldn't be back until later on in the evening.

At about five o'clock in the evening, Charlie stood up, shoved the scrap of paper he was writing on into his pocket and slouched downstairs to the kitchen. About five minutes later Neil closed his magazine and got up from the sofa. Then he too went into the kitchen. He met Kate outside the door. They glanced at each other but didn't say anything and then they both entered the kitchen. Charlie was sitting at the table in the kitchen reading a cardboard flyer, advertising a local takeaway pizza restaurant. He looked up and smiled weakly.

"Anyone for pizza?" he asked awkwardly. After spending a day in silence it felt strange to hear someone talking and Charlie's voice sounded hollow and seemed to echo off the bare stone walls of the old kitchen.

"Yeah, I wouldn't mind one," answered Neil in a slightly croaky voice which had been caused by him not talking to anyone all day. He cleared his throat.

"I'm starved."

"Me too," added Kate.

Suddenly it seemed as if a barrier had been broken. The teenagers relaxed and felt able to talk easily again and talk about trivial things once more.

"I wonder what's on telly?" pondered Neil.

"That comedy should be on tonight - you know, the first of the second series."

"Oh - I know what you mean - what's it called now?"

Chapter 6

"If you two want to watch some rubbish TV comedy again, I suppose I have no choice but to watch it with you," sighed Kate.

"Shall I order the pizza now?" asked Charlie.

"Hang on a mo' - what are you going to order?" asked Neil indignantly. "Don't we get a choice?"

"No," replied Charlie picking up the receiver and pretending to dial the number. He laughed as Neil launched himself at him and held the receiver as well as the phone out of Neil's reach. Neil climbed himself up Charlie and made a grab for the phone.

"Okay! Okay!" laughed Charlie, pushing Neil out of the way, "I haven't really rung them - what do you want?"

"Pepperoni with extra cheese!" cried Neil.

"The same," said Kate.

"Okay, I can live with that," said Charlie, whilst dialling the pizza takeaways number. Suddenly his face went white and he dropped the receiver and stood rooted to the spot, staring at nothing.

"What's up Charlie?" asked Kate in concern.

"He doesn't look well," said Neil. He picked up the receiver, which had cracked when it had hit the floor and put it to his ear. He frowned.

"There's no-one there - just the sound you get when the other person puts down the receiver on the other end."

"Who was it Charlie? What did they say?" asked Kate frantically shaking him at the same time. Charlie just swayed slightly. Kate pushed him gently onto a chair and said to Neil:

"My God! I've never seen him this bad before - what did they say Charlie?"

Charlie blinked once or twice and shook his head. The colour slowly came back to his cheeks and he said:

"Someone wants me dead," in a flat and monotonous voice.

"What?!" demanded Neil.

"Someone - a man I think - said to me: 'Charlie, you stick your nose into anything that doesn't concern you and you won't live to see the next day - the same goes if you tell anyone else.' "

"What did he mean?" asked Kate.

"I think I know." began Neil.

"The voice," interrupted Charlie, "the voice sounded familiar, as if I'd heard it somewhere before."

"Think Charlie, who was it?" asked Kate.

"I don't know!" wailed Charlie, "but I know what the guy meant!"

Chapter 6

"So do I," said Neil.

"What did he mean?" demanded Kate.

"You mean you don't know?" asked Charlie in surprise, "You really don't know?"

"No I don't," replied Kate, "Oh - unless you mean—" she looked into Charlie's eyes, and he nodded.

"Yes I do."

"Neil?" she asked, looking at Neil.

"I agree," he said.

"But that's crazy!" she cried, "There's no such thing as— " she paused.

"Go on - say it," urged Charlie.

"Ghosts."

"Oh come on Kate - wake up and smell the coffee! You've seen the evidence and you refuse to accept it! That bloke in the dining room - he wasn't a real person - he disappeared!"

"Also there was the diary in the loft - someone wants help," said Neil.

"I reckon," said Charlie, "and this is a long shot, but I reckon that someone was killed here and someone doesn't want us finding out."

Kate looked into Charlie's eyes and saw pure conviction in them.

"I agree," said Neil, "I think that we should find out who."

"But what about Charlie's threat?" asked Kate, becoming drawn into the discussion.

"I'll get by," said Charlie, "no worries."

Neil and Kate knew that Charlie was scared for his life, but that wasn't going to stop him. All they could do was follow him and help.

Chapter 7

*　　　　*　　　　*

Charlie was sitting at the window seat, looking out of the window at the oak tree. The oak tree was quite young and barely grew to the height of the second storey of the house. A shadow fell over him from behind. Charlie began to turn around when suddenly someone struck him with a crushing blow to the head and Charlie blacked out.

Charlie awoke. He was in the darkened room again, only this time the doorway was only half bricked up. Charlie could make out a dark square object behind the bearded figure bricking him in. The bearded face looked over the bricks and laughed at Charlie lying on the floor. Charlie tried to stand up and escape but he couldn't will his body to move. He felt as if he had been drugged. The face looked at Charlie again and grinned:

"So you're awake now you dirty piece of slime," the owner of the face said suddenly, looking at Charlie, "This'll teach yer."

The face grinned horribly. Charlie tried to stand up again, but he could only writhe about helplessly. He began writhing on the floor, but that was the most he could do. He hit his head against the rough stone floor in frustration and became unconscious.

Suddenly Charlie awoke up with a start. He was still in the room. The door to the room was almost fully bricked up. The stones were a dark red. The face glanced smugly into the room again and laughed before placing another brick onto the wall blocking up the door. Soon the last brick went in and the last shaft of flickering candle or lamp light disappeared and he was alone in the dark. He started calling for help, but his voice was muffled by the thick walls. He called again and again. He began to panic as his heart went into overdrive. He stood up and staggered forward. He hit a cold, hard wall and rebounded off it. He became disorientated as he staggered around the room, flailing his arms like a madman. He hit a corner and staggered backwards, out of control. He found another wall and started to beat against the stone, then he began to scrabble and try to dig his way trough with his finger nails whilst screaming to be let out. Charlie began to become dizzy as the air in the room grew stale and the oxygen ran out. He was slowly beginning to suffocate. Charlie stepped back and stopped screaming before suddenly collapsing to the floor as he passed out. He barely felt the hard ground. Before Charlie completely lost consciousness he heard demonic laughter echoing into the distance. Then his body went limp and Charlie lay unconscious on the floor as he slowly suffocated to death.

      *   *   *

Tap-tap-tap - tap-tap-tap - tap-tap-tap.

Charlie opened his eyes and scanned the room for the source of the noise. The door? No. The wardrobe? No. The window?

Tap-tap-tap. Went the oak's branch, banging against the window as the tree was shaken by the wind. As the wind blew through the eaves it made a shrill whistling sound as if a thousand ghosts were screaming in torment. Charlie shivered, despite the warmth of the bed as he remembered the dream and the part that hadn't dreamed before.

It was strange, he pondered, that when he had the dream it was so real that he didn't realise it was only a dream.

"Now, what was new?" he muttered to himself "The window seat - I was sitting there looking at the tree," he glanced up at the branches which were still tapping the window, "and suddenly a person hit me over the head."

Charlie shook his head in exasperation and climbed out of his bed. The house was comfortably warm when Charlie padded over the soft carpet to the bathroom.

After having a hot shower and a swift breakfast with Neil and Kate, Charlie brought up the subject of the ghost. He also mentioned the new part of his dream.

"I wonder what will happen next?" wondered Kate.

"I don't know, but I will next time I sleep." answered Charlie.

"Where shall we begin investigating your theory about a murder in the house Charlie?" asked Neil.

"The library of course," replied Charlie.

"Shall we leave now?" asked Kate.

"Yes - I'll quickly tell Mum and Dad," said Charlie.

The teenagers arrived at the library by ten o'clock. They went straight to the newspaper section.

The teenagers were taken aback at the amount of file cabinets in the section. A prim female librarian arrived behind them and asked them if they needed any help.

"We are trying to find any missing or murdered person reports for a school project," bluffed Charlie using the fail-safe excuse as a cover up for the teenagers' real reasons.

"What an awful project subject," muttered the librarian, "The headlines are in the newspaper viewer over there, but you'll probably find it easier to find what you are looking for on our new computer system."

She led the way to a computer at a desk in the corner and opened up the newspaper database.

"You just have to type in the word you are interested in and the computer comes up with whatever articles contain that word. You can also specify which dates you want to search between. Do you understand what to do?"

"We're fine," answered Charlie, "thanks."

"If you need any help I'll be over here," said

the librarian smiling slightly and walking out of the room.

Charlie typed in murder and waited for the computer to search out any articles. It came back with four articles, but these were not related to their house.

"Try missing," suggested Kate.

"Okay," said Charlie, typing the word in.

One hundred and sixty articles were found with reference to the word missing.

"This is hopeless," said Neil, "Can't we narrow it down a bit?"

"We could if we knew any dates," said Charlie, "Hang on! I've got it!"

"What?" asked Kate.

"The oak tree in my dream didn't reach my bedroom window by a few feet, but this morning I woke up to the sound of one of its branches tapping my window!"

"That must put it back to about eighty years," said Neil.

"Great!" exclaimed Charlie.

He specified dates between 1900 and 1920 and sat back to watch the results come up on the screen.

"There are thirty articles with the word missing in them," said Charlie.

"That would be because of the war," replied Kate, "Which ones are missing persons who disappeared locally?"

"There are five," answered Charlie, "Three are about a missing children who have run away from home, another is a missing woman and the last is a missing man"

"The man's from our house!" cried Kate suddenly, after reading the screen over Charlie's shoulder, "I don't believe it, but it's true!"

Even Charlie was shocked. He quickly printed the article out, folded it up and stuffed it into his pocket to look at in more detail later. As the teenagers left they thanked the librarian and made their way out. They discussed the article on the way home. Charlie pulled it out of his pocket for a more in-depth read. He then relayed the information he had read in the article to Neil and Kate:

"It says that the guy who went missing was aged forty-nine and was a teacher," he said. "Then, one day he didn't turn up at the school and never returned. People searched his house but found no sign of him. He seemed to have disappeared."

"Perhaps he was bricked in a room in the house like in your dream?" suggested Kate.

"But wouldn't someone have noticed a bricked up room?" asked Neil.

"The article says that he led a solitary lifestyle," replied Charlie. "Anyone searching his house after he disappeared wouldn't have noticed a missing room."

"But what about the new bricks and fresh concrete?" Neil continued.

"The murderer could have painted over the bricks or put up a wooden panel to cover up the brick work," Charlie answered.

"I think that we should search the house for any old rooms," stated Kate.

"But what will we find if we do discover the room?" asked Neil, leaving the question hanging in the air.

"We'll leap that hurdle when we reach it," said Charlie. "For now I think that we should search the house."

"How should we go about it?" asked Kate.

"I think that we should search downstairs only," said Charlie.

"Why?" asked Neil.

"Because," answered Charlie, "the teacher guy was bricked into a room that had a stone floor."

"Oh yeah," said Neil, slapping his hand against his forehead.

Chapter 7

"Anyway, we should go around the house tapping the wooden walls and listening out for a thud instead of a hollow sound to indicate a brick wall behind them. Then we can ... I don't know what we can do. We can't exactly just tear down a panel from a wall to see if there are bricks behind it."

"We could take a panel down carefully," suggested Neil.

"That's true," replied Charlie.

"What if the teacher was bricked in and the wall was painted over - we've got as many brick walls downstairs as we have non-brick walls." said Kate suddenly.

"Well, if we don't find anything suspicious after we have tapped all the panels in the house, we can then look for irregular brickwork - perhaps in the shape of a doorway."

"I think we should do that first actually," said Neil.

"You're right Neil," said Charlie, "That'll be easier to look out for."

"What if we don't turn up anythin?" asked Neil.

"Then we'll have to look again," replied Charlie, "Tonight I'll try to remember anything I see through the doorway in my dream."

"That's a good idea," said Kate. "So when shall we start our search?"

"Today," Charlie replied, his voice suddenly sounding cold, "I'm determined to sort this matter out, even if it kills me."

The children went silent, as they suddenly remembered the voice from the night before on the telephone they suddenly had a chilling thought that Charlie's words might come back to haunt him.

Chapter 8

The children didn't feel like being alone in the house anymore, so they decided the test all of the downstairs walls together. They started in the kitchen and began examining the walls intently. This took about ten minutes and they found nothing. They searched the dining room and the lounge but they did not find any irregular brickwork.

"This is hopeless," said Neil despondently, "we haven't found anything."

"We have only just begun the search," said Charlie attempting to lift the mood, "we have to search the wooden walls still."

"I'm beginning to wonder if we haven't just been acting stupidly all along and there is no ghost," Kate sighed.

"Look," began Charlie, "I've told you, this is no wild goose chase."

"Do you really think that?" asked Neil.

"Yes!" answered Charlie, "I damn well do!"

The teenagers spent the next hour examining every wooden and plaster wall in the house with no success. It seemed to them that they were on a wild goose chase after all as they neared the end of their search.

They were in Dad's study and were searching the last wall.

"Hang on," cried Charlie, "I think I've got it!" his triumphant grin fell as he realised that it wasn't the correct wall after all - it was another outside wall.

He sat down on a chair and rested his chin on his fist.

"I don't understand it," he sighed, "We've looked everywhere and we still haven't found anything!"

Kate sat opposite him and also sighed.

"I really thought we were onto something," she said, "but it turns out there's nothing."

"Hey - I've got it!" Neil cried, "I've got it!"

"What Neil," asked Charlie wearily.

"I had it once too, but I took pills and it went away," said Kate with a weary smile.

Chapter 8

"Don't be stupid Kate - I know what we've missed!" Neil shouted.

"Which is?" she asked him.

"We forgot to look behind furniture!"

Charlie and Kate looked at each other in disbelief.

"I can't believe we were so stupid!" Charlie said, "Well done Neil."

"Lets get searching then," said Kate.

"Before we start searching again," Neil said slowly, "I think that we should decide why we are looking for the room."

Charlie sat there for a few seconds before saying:

"So we have evidence that the teacher guy really was bricked in - then we can go about searching for a way to lay this ghost to rest before he drives me mad with these damn dreams!"

"Okay, now we know why we are doing this we can go about doing it," said Neil in a satisfied voice.

It didn't take long. After pulling an antique stack of shelves carefully away from the wall so the things on it wouldn't fall off, the teenagers found what they were looking for.

"It must have been the old larder," Charlie decided.

"I wonder who put the teacher guy in there?" asked Kate

"From what I remember the murderer was bearded with a slender and pale face."

"What sort of beard?" asked Neil.

"You know that president of America - what's his name?"

"Abraham Lincoln?" suggested Neil.

"That's him, yes the guy had a beard like Abraham Lincoln."

"That could have been anyone," sighed Kate.

"Perhaps my next dream will tell me who it was." said Charlie.

"Perhaps." said Neil dubiously.

"It's funny though," said Charlie as he helped Neil put the stack of shelves back.

"What is?" asked Neil.

"The voice on the phone - it was so familiar yet I can't put a finger on it, I really can't."

That night the teenagers watched television until eleven o'clock before going to bed. Charlie felt apprehensive as he slipped beneath the covers and it was a long time before he went to sleep.

Chapter 9

*   *   *

Charlie awoke. He was crouching in a dimly lit room looking over what appeared to be a desk. He could hear what sounded like chanting. Charlie went onto hands and knees and crawled to the edge of the desk and peered around: nothing - only flickering light. Charlie could smell some sort of incense. It wafted up his nostrils and became chokingly thick. Charlie began to feel dizzy and shook his head to get rid of the feeling. He then crept to the next corner of the desk and peered around it: five shadowy, robed and hooded figures were standing at each point of a pentagram - a five-sided star. Each figure held a candle and each figure chanted something in a language Charlie couldn't understand - perhaps it was Latin? He wondered.

The figures were focusing on the pentogram intently. Suddenly a sixth figure entered the room, carrying what appeared to be a chicken. The chicken did not act frightened and Charlie guessed it was drugged. The figure held the chicken by the neck in one hand and a long, slightly curved dagger in the other hand. The figure dropped the chicken onto a wooden block and next to a thick book on a lectern. The figure stood before the lectern and chanted several paragraphs of words before raising the dagger in both hands above its head. The hood fell away as the hands went up revealing a mans face with a Lincoln beard. The man's teeth were showing, tightly gripped together in front of thin, curled back lips, before the dagger dropped down at an almighty arc.

Charlie ducked back from the desk and grimaced as he heard a "thunk" sound and a wretched gurgle from the mouth of the chicken. Charlie poked his head around the desk again and watched in terror and amazement as a blood red swirling mist seeped from the wound in the chicken's bloodied neck. The mist seemed to be sucking towards the pentagram where it became a twisting column which spun like a miniature whirlwind. The red lit the faces of the chanters but not the bearded man. The bearded man had put the hood back over his head, but Charlie could distinctly see two yellow ovals beneath the hood, where the man's eyes should have been. The man began chanting something different to the others. His voice became deep and otherworldly - like a demon. The man's voice became louder and louder and more and more distorted until Charlie couldn't believe it was a man speaking. Suddenly the man looked at one of the figures on one corner of the pentagram and said in an almighty and evil voice:

"You don't truuuuely be-lieeeve."

The robed chanter stammered in return in a man's voice:

"I d-do Lord."

"BEGONE!" shouted the man whom Charlie decided had to be the leader.

Two orange and flaming beams of light from the leader's yellow, glowing eyes tore across the room and hit the disbeliever at his feet. The beams swept slowly up the person's body, vaporising it as it went until only the head remained, floating in the air with a twisted expression on it's face. Charlie wished the hood hadn't fallen off so the face could still be hidden.

The body-less head was screaming for mercy and screaming in pain before the beams of light suddenly stopped and the lead figure said to another chanter:

"Stick it on a spike and put it in my museum."

As the chanter picked it up, the head screamed for mercy again and again, but it's cries fell on deaf ears as the chanter took it away.

The lead figure laughed at the cries and said:

"Let him suffer forever in torment! Let his cries go unheard! Let his eternal pain and eternal suffering go as a lesson to you all! Now leave! And remember not too leave anything behind or you will suffer immensely."

The figure suddenly stopped in the process of leaving before he turned back and said:

"May I also let you be reminded not to tell anyone what happened here tonight, unless you want your spirit to live in torment forever!"

Charlie felt as if the person was talking to him directly and shuddered.

Ten minutes later, all of the shadowy figures had left, the last having blown the candles out.

Chapter 9

For the next ten minutes Charlie sat in darkness until he felt sure that it was safe to stand up and leave. He wondered where he was as he quickly opened a window and climbed out. He had forgotten to check which storey he was on in his fear, but fortunately it was ground floor. When Charlie had climbed out he turned around to close the window. After doing so he crept from the building and looked for a way out of the grounds. The area seemed familiar - suddenly he realised - it was his school! The new building wasn't there but the old one was the same as it had always been. The teacher must have discovered the Black Magic which was being practised by these people and was going to report it, Charlie decided, but one of the people had killed him before he had had a chance to. So the bearded man must have been talking to me, Charlie decided. The man had the same voice as the phone voice and also looked the same as the murderer, Charlie thought.

Charlie sighed as he made his way back to the house under the full moon, unhappy in the knowledge of what would happen next. When he got in, he went straight to the dining room to sit down and think. The dining room was dark, so he lit a candle with a box of matches nearby, before sitting at the window seat. Before long he had dozed off into dreamless sleep.

Charlie awoke. He was still sitting at the window seat. He looked out of the window at the oak tree. The oak tree was quite young and barely grew to the height of the second storey of the house. A shadow fell over him from behind. Charlie knew who it was but still began to turn round to see the person. Suddenly the person struck him with a crushing blow to the head and Charlie blacked out.

Charlie awoke. He was in the darkened room again. The doorway was half bricked up. Charlie tried to make out the dark square object behind the bearded figure bricking him in and realised that it was the shelf. The bearded face looked over the bricks and laughed at Charlie lying on the floor. Charlie tried to stand up and escape but he couldn't will his body to move. He felt as though he had been drugged. The face looked at Charlie again and grinned:

"So you're awake now you dirty piece of slime," the owner of the face sneered, looking at Charlie, "This'll teach yer."

The owner of the face was the same person from earlier on at the school.

Chapter 9

Charlie tried to stand up again, this time gaining some movement. He began writhing on the floor, but that was the most he could do. He accidentally hit his head against the rough stone floor and became unconscious.

Suddenly Charlie awoke up with a start. He was still in the room. By now he knew exactly what to expect. Charlie sighed reluctantly at the thought of going through the same thing all over again.

*　　　　*　　　　*

Chapter 10

Charlie sat up, suddenly wide awake. He looked around himself and saw that he was in his bedroom. He relaxed then tensed again as he remembered his dream - no nightmare.

Charlie shivered and climbed out of bed. He went into the bathroom straight away and had a quick wash, before having breakfast downstairs in the kitchen.

"Morning Charlie!" greeted Kate, coming into the kitchen. She saw the pallid look on Charlie's face and frowned, "What's up?" she asked.

Charlie looked at her and Kate suddenly knew what was wrong.

"The dream?" she questioned Charlie.

"Yeah," he replied sullenly.

"What happened?" Kate asked inquisitively.

"I don't want to talk about it for the moment thanks," answered Charlie.

Kate decided not to ask anymore questions for the time being and made herself some breakfast. She sat opposite Charlie and together they ate in silence. They had both finished when Neil came in.

"Morning people!" he said cheerfully. He looked at Charlie and sighed: "You had that dream again?"

"Yeah," Charlie sighed again.

"Poor you - what happened?"

"I'll tell you later Neil," said Charlie, raising his voice slightly.

"Okay, okay," Neil said, "I was just asking."

"Just don't okay?" Charlie growled.

"God, what's up with him?" sneered Neil.

"Drop it Neil," said Kate, "Don't annoy him."

"Fine!" Neil retorted, storming out of the kitchen.

"Damn! Damn! Damn!" cursed Charlie "What have I done?"

"Don't worry Charlie," soothed Kate, "he'll get over it - he's just hurt that you were so hostile to him, that's all."

"I should have told him," Charlie said, "Oh well - perhaps later?"

"Okay," said Kate, "It's up to you."

Charlie spent the rest of the morning and some of the afternoon reading, watching television and writing. At about half past three he went to find Neil and Kate. He found them in Neil's bedroom playing on the computer.

"Hi," greeted Kate, looking up when Charlie entered, "Damn!" she suddenly cried as she looked back at the screen, "You made me crash!"

"That's your excuse Kate," jaunted Neil.

"Hi," said Charlie, "Look, sorry Neil, I was just in a bad mood."

"Sorry about what?" asked Neil, looking up, "Damn! Now I've crashed."

"See, I told you he would get over it," grinned Kate.

"Whoops!" said Neil suddenly grinning, "I've only gone and accidentally pressed the RESET button!"

"You cheat," Kate cried out.

"I'm not a cheat, it was an accident."

"You did it because you were losing."

"Would I do that?" asked Neil, his face a picture of innocence.

"Oh well, I suppose we've spent too long on it anyway," said Kate.

"By the way," began Charlie, "I've been thinking about last night's dream since this morning and now I've sorted it out in my head I can now tell you what happened."

"Has anything new happened which throws a new light on our investigation?" asked Kate, suddenly serious.

"Sort of," answered Charlie, "But I do know one thing."

"What's that?" asked Neil.

"It must have been the worst damn dream in my life, and if that was what really happened to this teacher, then we are up against more than your everyday, lesser-spotted, common or garden haunted house."

Kate giggled slightly at what Charlie said, before asking:

"It was that bad?"

"Yes," replied Charlie, "and I'm going to tell you every little detail of it."

Charlie proceeded to tell his brother and sister about the dream. As Charlie told them it, they grew more and more horrified.

"You've got to be kidding!" said Neil in disbelief.

"I'm perfectly serious," replied Charlie.

"But it was only a dream." began Kate.

"Which just happens to contain stuff that has really happened so far," retorted Charlie. "So why shouldn't this be true?"

"Well, it sounds so made up," said Kate searching for the right words.

"So you can believe in ghosts, but not in this other stuff because this other stuff - Black Magic - sounds so made up," Charlie replied hotly, mimicking Kate's choice of words.

"Well, as much as I hate to believe him," Neil said, "it looks like we have no choice - everything else is true, so why not this?"

"Okay, I'll go along with you," Kate sighed, giving in, "but don't say I didn't tell you so if you are wrong."

Charlie looked at her, his eyes burning:

"I am right!"

"So what shall we do?" asked Neil.

"Lets go to our school and have a look around," answered Charlie.

"Which room did this ritual happen in?" asked Kate.

"Errr - I think it was a maths room - room 84" replied Charlie, "I think it's a senior teacher's room."

"Have you ever had lessons in there?" asked Neil.

"No - have you?"

"No," replied Neil.

"Nor me," shrugged Kate when the boys looked to her for an answer.

"So we know nothing about the room - none of us know anything strange about it," Charlie summarised.

"No, so we should find stuff out about it now," Neil said.

"Right now?" asked Kate.

"Yeah," replied Neil.

"Okay then," shrugged Kate, "Let's go."

Suddenly Dad burst into the room.

"What are you all plotting about?" he jested, and then before they could say anything he said: "I've got great news: I've just booked a few days at Aqualand."

"When do we leave?" asked Kate.

"Tomorrow morning."

"How long?"

"Until the end of half-term."

"Why so suddenly Dad?" asked Charlie.

"Because we need a rest after moving in - why, don't you want to go to Aqualand for a break?" Dad answered.

Chapter 10

"It's not that Dad - I personally want to go - it's just come as a bit of a surprise, that's all."

"Well, why don't you get packing then?" asked Dad.

"Alright," replied Charlie, "come on you two," he said, gesturing to his brother and sister.

Upstairs the teenagers met in Charlie's room.

"What shall we do Charlie?" asked Neil, "We're going to be back at school afterwards and we won't have time to investigate."

"You're forgetting something," said Charlie.

"What?" asked Neil,.

"We are going to be at school and therefore able to continue our investigation there."

"But what about anything we have to investigate out of the school?"

"Somehow," answered Charlie, "I don't think we are going to be investigating very much outside of school anymore."

"Why?" asked Kate.

"I just don't think we will be,"

Chapter 11

The teenagers had a great time at Aqualand and had time to forget all the worries of home life for a few days. Charlie stopped having the strange dream and he had his first good night's sleep in a week.

The family returned back home on Sunday night, happy and refreshed after their exhilarating holiday and prepared for the week ahead.

In the car on the way back to their house, Charlie thought about the ghost for the first time since they had left. Neil was asleep, his head resting against the window behind the driver's seat. Kate was sitting in the middle and was reading a magazine.

"Kate," Charlie said quietly.

"What?" she asked, looking at him quizzically.

"When we get back, I'm going to start getting those dreams again."

Kate considered this for a few moments before saying:

"So? We've nearly worked them out now, then we'll be able to find a way of solving them."

"Yeah, but after the last few nights, I don't think I can face the dreams again."

Kate looked straight at Charlie and said:

"You've got too." Charlie sighed and looked out of the window again, watching the hedgerows go whizzing past, and the streetlights which momentarily shone through before disappearing into the night.

Charlie closed his eyes. Within a few minutes he was sound asleep.

Charlie felt someone shaking him gently, and heard someone saying something. He heard it again and strained his ears to catch what the person was saying.

"Wake up Charlie."

He opened his eyes and saw Kate, shaking him whilst telling him to wake up.

"At last!" she exclaimed, "I was beginning

to think you'd never wake up - come on, we're going in."

"Charlie slowly climbed out of the car and looked at his watch. It was ten minutes past eleven.

Charlie picked up his satchel which was on the car floor, and went in, followed by Dad, who locked the car.

Inside, Charlie slowly climbed upstairs, his feet barely clearing each step.

"Would you like a cup of tea Charlie?" called Mum from downstairs.

"No-thank you Mum," he replied in a slurred voice.

He was surprised at how tired he was, and decided that it must have been all the activities he had done over the past few days.

He climbed into bed and within seconds was sound asleep.

*　　　　　*　　　　　*

Charlie awoke. He was standing at the entrance of the school, holding a big, heavy iron key in one hand. Charlie inserted the key into the door and turned it. The lock was well oiled and turned silently. Charlie pushed the heavy oak door open and stepped inside. He then quickly made his way along the corridor which led to the classroom in which the Black Magic ritual would surely take place. The corridor was cold and dark. Along one wall were ancient black and white photographs of all the headmasters the school had had over the years. Charlie idly looked at each one as he past them. He recognised most of the photographs, as they were still there to the present day.

Suddenly Charlie stopped in front of the last of the photographs and gasped. He couldn't believe it. The photograph on the wall was that of the bearded man who performed the ritual a few nights ago, who would do so again tonight. Charlie looked at the name on the brass plaque beneath the photograph.

'Edward P. Oates' 1905-. Charlie quickly memorised this before continuing along the corridor. He entered the room a minute later and went to the desk. On the desk was a folder entitled HOMEWORK. Charlie decided that this was what he must be here for. The teacher had obviously left it behind and had come back for it, only to discover the Black Magic taking place. Charlie hastily picked up the folder, but accidentally let it open, spilling the pages all over the floor. Charlie got down onto his knees and had just begun picking all the sheets up, when a person walked through the doorway, wearing a hooded robe. The figure was quickly followed by another, who was carrying something. Then, four others walked in, each carrying something, and began to set up the things they had brought with them. Candles were set upon tall candle sticks and were lit. One figure drew a precise pentogram with chalk onto the floor and then drew a perfect circle around it, which touched each of the five points.

Then the first figure left and the other five stood upon each point of the pentagram and began chanting. They had spoken nothing until now and Charlie jumped slightly when they began to chant. He put the folder down and sat with his back resting against the desk. He knew what was going to happen from here and he didn't like the thought of it one bit.

*   *   *

Charlie was awoken by the sound of his alarm clock ringing. Charlie groaned and climbed from his bed slowly.

Something was nagging him at the edge of his consciousness, but he couldn't quite grasp what. It had something to do with the dream. That was it - he had to remember something.

But what?

A name. Ed. Edward. Edward P. Oates, he remembered. What about Edward P. Oates though? The headmaster with the beard! That was it, he had to remember the name of Edward P. Oates from the dream. Edward P. Oates, headmaster from 1905.

When had he stopped being a headmaster? Charlie wondered, I suppose I'll have to find out today.

Charlie quickly got washed and clothed, before having breakfast. He was soon joined by Neil and Kate.

"Morning Charlie," greeted Neil.

"Morning," greeted Kate.

"Have a nice sleep?" asked Charlie.

"Fine," answered Neil.

"Great - and yourself?" asked Kate

"Had that dream again," replied Charlie.

"Was it bad?" inquired Kate, pouring her milk onto her cornflakes.

"The new stuff wasn't, but I re-dreamed that bit I had a couple of nights ago," Charlie answered.

"Ouch," empathised Neil, "it must be awful dreaming the same terrible thing again and again and again.

Chapter 11

"It is," replied Charlie, "but I found something new out which is pretty bad."

"What?" Kate asked.

"Listen and I will tell you." said Charlie.

Charlie then told his brother and sister about his dream, especially the bit about the photo and the name.

"D' you know what's really strange though?" Charlie said, "You know I said the bearded guy - Oates - looked familiar."

"Yes," said Neil.

"Well, he still looks familiar but I can't quite put my finger on it," continued Charlie.

"What do you mean?" asked Kate, "He looked familiar because of the photo on the wall - that's where you've seen him before."

"That's the thing, he doesn't look familiar because of the picture - I've seen his face somewhere else before but I can't remember where,"

Neil and Kate mulled this over for a while before Neil said:

"I wish you'd remember Charlie, for your own sake."

Chapter 12

The teenagers left for school at half past eight and arrived at five minutes to nine, just five minutes before their registration bell. Neil and Kate were in the same tutor group, but Charlie wasn't, so he left them as they entered the building.

When he entered class, he went over to his group of friends and began talking to them. They talked for a few minutes about the half-term holiday and what they had done, before the bell went and they sat down in readiness for the register. Ten minutes later Charlie went to his first lesson, which was maths. Afterwards he had English, French and art.

After lunch there was a school assembly. Charlie was near the front of the hall with some of his friends. He normally sat at the back but this week seating arrangements had changed. A teacher stood at the front of the hall and tried to get everyone's attention. Finally, after the last few conversations ended, the Headmaster walked in and stood in front of the lectern at the front, his hands firmly clasping the edge of it. The Headmaster spoke with a stern tone and pronounced each syllable with precision.

The Headmaster never seemed to laugh or smile when he was in school, although Charlie had heard rumours about him smiling once. Charlie didn't believe the rumours himself.

Since being at the school, Charlie had never really seen the Headmaster up close. The Headmaster seemed to keep himself distant from the pupils and was never really seen about school apart from when he took assemblies. When in assembly, Charlie could never really make out the Headmaster's face that well, due to the fact that the Headmaster was at the front and Charlie normally sat at the back.Now, Charlie could see the headmaster close up.

The Headmaster had narrow and gaunt features - his hair was brown and his chin was shaven. The Headmaster's lips were very thin - almost to the point of non-existence.

Chapter 12

As the headmaster droned on about this week's subject - the lack of discipline in schools nowadays - Charlie had a haunting feeling. The Headmaster's face, his voice, they both nagged at Charlie, taunting him, hinting at something which Charlie could not quite grasp.

Suddenly Charlie worked it out. The revelation came suddenly, as if a switch had flicked in his brain. He hadn't believed it before because it had seemed so ridiculous, but now he easily made the connection.

The Headmaster was Edward P. Oates, the old headmaster.

Charlie frowned. The Headmaster no longer had a beard but looked the same age as the person in the dream so he couldn't be.

Or perhaps that was part of the Black Magic? Perhaps the Headmaster wanted eternal life?

Charlie knew Edward Oates was a witch - wasn't that something to do with the Devil? There were stories about selling your soul for things like that, so perhaps that was what Edward had done?

A friend suddenly nudged Charlie:

"Come on Charlie," the friend said, "assembly's over - it's time for science."

"Okay," replied Charlie, grasping one last

look at the Headmaster before he left the hall, "I'm coming."

After school, Charlie met up with Neil and Kate.

"Tell me I'm crazy," he said.

"You're crazy," said Neil.

"Ha Ha Neil, anyway call me crazy but," he said catching Neil's eye, "I think I know who the person is that Oates reminds me of."

"Who?" asked Kate.

Charlie told Neil and Kate about assembly and how sure he was that he was correct. When he finished, Kate said:

"Charlie, that's the stupidest thing I have heard for ages."

"Are you sure Kate?" asked Charlie. "You're forgetting that you are on a ghost hunt."

Kate sighed and said:

"So what shall we do now?"

"We'll quickly pop back and sneak a look at the corridor photos."

"Fine," answered Kate.

Back in school they made their way into the hall with all of the school's headmasters. There were still pupils walking around the campus so they didn't look out of place.

They reached Edward's photograph and

Neil and Kate had a good look at it. After this photograph there were eight others.

"Oh my God!" gasped Charlie, having moved on to look at the other photographs, "Look at them!"

Neil and Kate quickly came looked at the next eight photographs and studied them carefully for a while, not finding anything which was particularly out of the ordinary with them. Then, first Neil, then Kate, they got it.

"I don't believe it," cried Kate, her words streaming out of her mouth at a rapid pace.

"That's damn freaky," Neil said in a quivering voice.

"You can see it too then?" asked Charlie.

"Of course we can," replied Neil, "The headmasters are all the same person."

"There are slight differences obviously," surmised Charlie, "But the eyes, cheekbones and thin lips give it away."

"I'm surprised nobody noticed," said Neil.

"So am I," said Charlie, "But I suppose it is because we were scrutinising the photos carefully."

"So this means that these headmasters are really just old Ed."

"I wonder if any other photos before

Edward's are the same man?" asked Kate.

"No," replied Neil, "Edward Oates is the first."

"I wonder who the other people are?" asked Charlie, "I get the feeling that they may just be senior teachers or something."

"I don't want to think of it," said Kate shivering.

"Still," said Neil in false cheerfulness, "at least it explains why all the senior staff are so freaky - they're all witches!"

"Ha, Ha, Neil, you really are so funny," said Charlie sarcastically.

"I wish we went to a normal school," Kate sighed. "All schools cannot be like this."

"They're not - we're just the unlucky ones," answered Charlie. "Anyway, let's make our way home now - I'm starving."

Chapter 13

Back home, their parents were not back from work yet, so they made themselves some thick and creamy hot chocolate topped with spray cream. To round this off they each took a few biscuits from the tin and went into the lounge. They settled their cups onto the coffee table and switched on the television.

There was nothing on the television which was of interest to the teenagers so they sat and talked for a while. Then Charlie decided to do some more work on his story, which hehad neglected of late. The extra writing which appeared when Charlie was asleep had stopped since the teenagers had begun to investigate so Charlie was surprised to find a new entry.

He quickly showed it to his brother and sister.

The boy and his helpers were in danger - the witch knew everything and was now out to silence them so they would not tell others of the actions of the witchand his acolytes.

"What's an acolyte?" asked Kate.

"A sort of assistant," Charlie told her.

"This is a warning," stated Charlie.

"A warning?" asked Neil in surprise.

"Yes, it's obvious," replied Charlie.

"Oh, I see," Neil said, realising it suddenly, "I don't know how I missed that."

"Well what shall we do?" asked Kate.

"Stay inside and be careful."

"I'm scared Charlie," stated Kate matter-of-factly

"Look, we'll pull through Kate," Charlie told her.

"I hope so Charlie, I hope so." Kate said. "Let's talk about something else."

Later on, at six o'clock, the teenagers parents rang to say that they were staying away for the night, and told the teenagers to make themselves something for dinner. They ate microwave lasagne, which their mother always had in the freezer for such times as this.

Afterwards they watched a television comedy show before going to bed early for once.

Soon they were all asleep, cosy in their separate beds.

For once Charlie did not have his dream, but he slept fitfully.

Suddenly he awoke with a start and sat up. He had heard his name being called. He looked around but saw nothing, so he slowly rested his head upon his pillow again and closed his eyes. Suddenly he heard it again. He sat up again and looked around for the source of the voice. The wind was blowing through the eaves outside and Charlie listened to it carefully. It sounded like someone whispering: "Charlie, Charlie," again and again.

Charlie grinned to himself and wiped the cold sweat from his forehead before laying his head upon the pillow again.

Charlie frowned. If the wind was blowing he should have been hearing the oak tree tapping the window. Also he should be able to see it shaking in the moonlight. He sat up again and looked out of the window at the still tree. Slowly, horror began to crawl through his body and a cold chill ran up his spine. The words on his pad came back to haunt him.

Kate awoke. She felt someone's hand over

her face. She opened her eyes but there was nothing. She decided that she had imagined it and tried to get back to sleep. Suddenly she felt it again. She opened her eyes - nothing. Then she saw a man-shaped shadow in the corner and opened her mouth to scream.

Neil opened his eyes slowly. He heard a creak of a floorboard. He looked in the direction, thinking perhaps Charlie or Kate was there. Nobody. He shut his eyes again and decided that it must have been the floorboards settling. Suddenly he heard a shuffling sound on the other side of the bed. He opened his eyes again and looked in the sound's direction - nothing. Just before he closed his eyes again he saw a shadow in front of the window and then heard a loud scream, coming from Kate's bedroom.

Charlie was about to switch his bedside light on when he heard Kate scream. He leapt from bed and ran out of the room.

In the corridor Neil and Charlie met, looked at each other briefly and ran towards Kate's door, just as Kate ran out of it.

Charlie and Neil stopped and dragged Kate down the corridor and downstairs by her arms.

"What's wrong Kate?" asked Charlie, "Why did you scream?"

Chapter 13

"There was someone in my bedroom," replied Kate.

"Yours too?" asked Neil, "There was someone in mine as well."

"And mine," said Charlie

"A person in each of our rooms!" Neil cried. "Where did they come from?"

"I think they are something to do with the warning," Charlie explained, "I think that it was witchcraft or black magic."

"You mean they weren't really there?" asked Kate.

"I think that we will find no-one if we return - I reckon that Oates is toying with us."

"Then what shall we do?" asked Kate.

"Stop him."

"How?" asked Neil.

"We go to the school."

"What, now?" asked Kate.

"Yes, now."

"All of us?"

"Yes, we'll be just as unsafe here if the guy is using magic - we'll need all the people we can to stop him,"

"I'm in," said Neil.

"So am I," said Kate.

"So let's go!" Charlie exclaimed.

Chapter 14

"Charlie?" asked Kate.

"What?," Charlie answered.

"We need clothes, to wear to the school."

"Good point," Charlie said thoughtfully. "If you want, I'll go upstairs and grab our clothes and come straight back down."

"I'll come too," Neil said.

"No," Charlie replied, "you stay here with Kate."

"If you're sure." Neil said doubtfully.

"Look, I'll be fine!" Charlie told him. "Now I'm off upstairs - you two find anything that we'll need to help us - torches for example."

"Okay Charlie," Kate said. "Be careful."

"I'm only going upstairs," Charlie said over his shoulder as he trod on the first step. It

x

creaked ominously. "It's not as if anything's going to happen."

Charlie continued cautiously upstairs until he reached the landing. He pressed the light switch. Click! Nothing. Click! Click!

Charlie shrugged and proceeded down the corridor slowly. He was trying to convince himself that the light-bulb had probably just blown and that there was nothing spooky about that. He didn't find himself very convincing.

He went into his bedroom and pressed the light switch. Again nothing. There was a bright blue flash at the window and then there was an enormously loud rumble which seemed to shake the house to its very foundations. Charlie jumped in fright and then forced himself to relax.

Thunder and lightning, that's all it is, he said to himself as he grabbed his clothes and ran into Kate's room. He grabbed her clothes from her chair where she had left them as another bolt of lightning flashed outside, followed by another almighty thunder roll. He went into Neil's room and picked up Neil's jeans, pullover and T-shirt. As he picked the T-shirt up, he looked at the window. Thin curtains were drawn over the window, but Charlie could still see the blue of the lightning's flash through them. Two lightning bolts flashed, followed almost instantly by rumbles of thunder. Then a third flashed, illuminating a shady figure. The window went dark almost immediately again, before being illuminated once again by lightning. There was nothing there.

Charlie turned and ran towards the door, whilst still holding the clothes. The figure was in the doorway, with its hands outstretched. Charlie charged into it and head-butted it at the same time. As the figure fell back, Charlie kicked away its legs and ran down the stairs. The figure cursed as it rolled about on the floor. Lightning flashed, once, twice, three times, and the figure was gone.

Downstairs, Neil and Kate were waiting in the kitchen.

"I wonder what's keeping Charlie?" pondered Neil out loud.

"I don't know," replied Kate.

Suddenly there was a thump upstairs, followed by rapid footsteps echoing off of the stairs. Charlie burst in and lay against the table panting.

"Here," he said, gasping for breath, "are your clothes - put them on quick and let's go."

"What happened?" asked Kate in concern. "What was all that thumping?"

"I saw a man in the window and by the door - he tried to grab me," Charlie replied, recovering a little.

"We should leave as soon as possible," Neil said as he pulled on his jeans.

"Well I'm ready," Kate said.

"And so am I," said Charlie as he pulled his jumper over his head, "Come on Neil."

"I'm ready," Neil answered.

The teenagers crept towards the front door.

As they passed the hall cupboard on the way to the door, Neil stopped and opened it. He rummaged about inside until he pulled out a rounder bat.

"It's not as good as a baseball bat, but it'll do," he whispered to Charlie.

"Anything else in there?" asked Charlie in a hushed voice.

"I'll see," replied Neil. He once again began rummaging around in the cupboard until he found a cricket bat.

"I think there's another one as well," Neil said as he handed the bat to Charlie, "Ah, here it is."

He handed the bat to Kate who took it and weighed it up in her hands.

Chapter 14

"Thanks Neil," she answered, "Just what I need for combating the powers of darkness."

"At least it's something," Neil said, "It's better than nothing."

"Come on you two," Charlie said, pushing them forward.

The teenagers reached the front door, pulled their shoes on and slowly let themselves out. They walked down the garden path in the rain and opened the gate. It creaked loudly as it opened and the teenagers winced.

"Come on," whispered Charlie as they filed through the gateway, "Let's get cracking."

The teenagers quickly and quietly ran down the street in the direction of the school, peering furtively left and right, constantly alert to anything out of the ordinary.

Presently, they arrived at the school and climbed through the gap in fence which was situated in the middle of the school field. The field was muddy from the rain and in places the mud had turned to liquid. The teenagers slipped and slid over the field in their trainers which didn't grip in the slightest.

They finally reached the playground and made their way to the old school building. They walked along the wall testing the windows to see if any opened. After about three minutes they found one. It shuddered open and the teenagers quickly climbed in, one after another, each wielding his or her weapon. Once in, they weaved silently through the rows of chairs before reaching the door. Charlie opened the door a fraction and they went through in single file.

"Follow me and keep close to the wall," Charlie whispered to his brother and sister.

"Okay," replied Neil and Kate together.

The building was completely silent, except for the sound of the quiet footsteps of the teenagers, which could be heard if you listened very carefully.

As they approached the room, they began to see a pale, yellow, flickering light. When they reached the door, they found that the light was coming from within and was shining through the glass panel in the upper half of the door. The light darkened occasionally as a person within the room moved past the light's source.

Faint murmuring could be heard from within the room as well as a voice which was slightly louder than the rest. It appeared to be chanting something. There were several bright flashes and a strange clicking, rattling sound was heard, which slowly died away, leaving just the murmuring and chanting again.

Charlie motioned for Neil and Kate to stay where they were and slowly moved forward so that he could just peer in through the glass.

Inside was the scene from his dream, just how he remembered it. There were candles of the thick yellow variety, there was a pentagram on the floor with a hooded and robed figure on each corner and there was the sixth figure - the headmaster.

Inside the pentogram some sparks suddenly began to appear - white sparks which slowly multiplied until there was a fiery column of bright, white, sparking light. Blue light flashed within the centre of the column.

The headmaster raised his hands above his head and chanted something in a loud voice. An image slowly began to form within the column of light and Charlie began to make out three figures. Two were crouching next to each other and a third was leaning forward, peering through something.

It was them, Charlie suddenly realised, the image was of he and his brother and sister crouching in the corridor.

Charlie said to Neil:

"Right, let's go in - they're on to us!"

"Stay there Kate," Neil said.

"No way - I'm going in."

"No, don't - it's too dangerous."

"I don't care," she replied.

"Now," cried Charlie.

He tore open the door and ran in, followed by Neil and Kate, who had decided to go in despite Neil's advice.

Charlie ran into one of the figures and pushed the figure into the middle of the pentagram. The figure turned black before disappearing with a flash of light.

Neil meanwhile had hit one of the figures over the head with his bat. The figure staggered forward before collapsing on the floor, unconscious. Kate had also hit someone with her cricket bat. The figure stumbled a little and fell, its hood falling from its head. The figure was a woman. Kate instantly recognised her. It was the head of the mathematics department - Mrs. Briggs.

"My ankle - it's twisted," she cried.

"My God, what are you doing?" exclaimed Kate "Why are you doing this?"

Mrs. Briggs looked up at Kate with anger on her face.

"Kate, what are you doing here, what you are doing is against school rules!"

"And what your doing isn't?" asked Kate in disgust, before turning away and hitting at waist height someone who was about to grab her. The person collapsed onto the floor, writhing in agony.

At this time, Charlie had just hit someone with a chair, having lost his bat in the column of light. The person whom he had just hit staggered backwards into the wall and sliding down.

During all this the headmaster had remained calm. Now, he raised his right hand into the air and muttered something. Sulphur coloured fire burst forth from his fingertips and spiralled towards Neil. He raised his rounder bat and shielded himself. The bat burnt instantly and turned to ash.

"Ouch!" cried Neil, leaping behind the desk at the front of the classroom.

Kate ran towards the headmaster with her bat raised. The headmaster raised an eyebrow. Kate was lifted from her feet and pinned halfway up the opposite wall. The headmaster laughed and looked around for Charlie, who had just made it out of the door. A trial of yellow fire followed him and burst against the wall in the corridor. Leaving the wall with a red hot circle which glowed and curled the paint.

"I'll get you later, foo-ool boy," hissed the headmaster in a fearsome voice, unlike any human voice.

Neil furtively opened drawers behind the desk in search of a weapon - any weapon. He tore a drawer right out and hurled it over the desk in the shallow hope that it may just hit the raving head-teacher. It did, with a heavy thud which sent the headmaster staggering, but unfortunately didn't stop or injure him. The headmaster raised his hand to emit another fireball, this time at the desk. The fireball ripped through the air with a terrible sizzling, roaring noise. The fireball was a round ball of blue this time. It hit the desk and bathed it in a soft, blue bubble of light, which shrank until it moulded around the desk. Neil kicked himself away, just in time. All the corners and edges of the desk became outlined in thin lines of dazzling orange, before the entire desk exploded with an almighty force, which blasted Neil back against the wall, knocking him unconscious. The headmaster left Neil for dead and quickly left the room in search of Charlie.

Chapter 14

Charlie meanwhile was on his way to the science section of the school. He burst into the first science room he came across and went over the row of cupboards in the corner. He opened them one by one, but they contained only retort stands, conical flasks and other such things.

"Damn," exclaimed Charlie quietly, "They're in the preparation room."

Charlie left straight away, to make his way to the preparation room at the end of the corridor.

The room was quiet for a moment, the cupboard doors open. One remained swinging slightly from where Charlie had opened it in his haste. On the opposite wall, a shape began pushing through the plaster. The shape was a face. A giant face. The face began to take the shape of the headmaster's, but completely white. Suddenly the eyes became real and they looked around the room. The head stretched the wall as it peered left and right before sinking back into the plaster, until nothing was left, except a plain white, flat wall.

The headmaster stalked along the corridor, the darkness presenting no barrier as he pursued Charlie. He closed his eyes for a moment, muttered and then opened them again. The eyes seemed to be looking at things other than what was ahead of him. He turned his head left and then right as if peering around himself, before he closed his eyes and muttered a few more words. He opened his eyes again and this time they were normal.

"So that's what he's up to is he?," the Headmaster muttered in his inhuman voice, "How innnnteresting."

And the headmaster's eyes glowed in the dark. They glowed yellow.

Charlie burst into the preparation room in a near panic. He had wasted too much time already, he knew it. Charlie fumbled around drawers, looking for chemicals. He found a drawer with a pot of blue powder. Copper something-or-other. He didn't have time to look. He rapidly opened other drawers, until he came across what he wanted. Potassium.

From what Charlie remembered from his science lessons, potassium was very reactive with water and air, which was the reason it was generally stored in kerosene. If Charlie used what was in this drawer, he might just defeat the headmaster.

Charlie took out of the drawer ten jars filled with kerosene with lumps of potassium in the bottom of each. Charlie hastily unscrewed the jars and picked up some tweezers. He then picked up each lump and transferred it into one of the jars. He decided that he must have about half a kilo in all - enough? He hoped so. He filled up a tray of water and set it upon the floor in the corridor just before the doorway. Charlie then filled up a bucket with water and covered the floor as a precaution - just in case things went wrong he needed as much water as possible to react with the potassium.

Charlie knew that he was working a long shot but he had to have a go anyway - anything to stop the crazy headmaster from getting him. He wondered how his brother and sister were getting on and hoped that the headmaster had followed him and left them alone.

Suddenly, Charlie heard a shuffling sound in the corridor. He held the open jar in his hand and prayed silently to himself, and hoped that someone was listening to his prayers.

There was a splash and a curse, and the shuffling stopped. Charlie leapt from inside the preparation room and poured the potassium into the tray of water in which the headmaster was standing, eyes glowing fearsome yellow.

"Bye sir!" quipped Charlie and ran away,

down the corridor as the potassium fiercely burnt in the water. The headmaster's robe set alight and soon he was engulfed in a human fireball. Except the headmaster wasn't human. He may once have been, but not now. No, now he was the very Devil himself.

Oh well, Charlie said to himself in a half crazed way, I hope he enjoys fire as much as they say he does.

There was a ear piercing scream from behind him. Charlie turned and gasped. The headmaster was growing - growing bigger and bigger. His robe ripped, revealing a bright red torso. The headmaster grew talons and his head grew distorted and ugly. His whole body was flame red.

"I wiillll gettttt youuu Charrr-lieee!" screamed the headmaster in rage, stepping through the charred ruins of the corridor.

Flames licked the ceiling and soon the heat grew unbearable. Charlie ran and ran, whilst fireballs whizzed by him from the enraged demon the headmaster had become. The headmaster laughed crazily, drunk with rage. His now wide and armoured shoulders scraped along the corridor walls, leaving long scratch marks in their wake.

Chapter 14

Charlie reached a door and had just got through when a dark green streak of fire burst violently against it, melting the glass panel and atomising the wood.

Charlie screamed and ran through another door, this one outside.

He ran like the wind across the school playground, feeling very exposed. If only he could find something - anything to fight this madman off of him.

Suddenly, Charlie tripped and stumbled and then tripped again. As he fell he twisted, and saw the demon towering above him, wrath glowing in its eyes. Long, black blades extended through the demon's charred hands.

"Yooouuu wiiillll nnnooottt diiiee quiiiicckkllllyyy!" the demon screeched, "Yooouuuu wiiillll diiee ssslllooowwwllllyy!"

Charlie closed his eyes for what he thought was the last time, trying to think of a final thing to say before he died - something heroic, but he couldn't.

"AAARRRGGGHH!" the demon screamed suddenly.

Charlie opened his eyes and looked up as the demon looked down at himself and then turned round to face Neil. Charlie could see

Neil through the demon. The demon was slowly disappearing. The former headmaster tried to strike Neil but his hand went harmlessly through him. The demon tried a spell but all that happened was a puff of smoke coming from beneath his finger nails. He looked at them in disbelief and then looked at Neil.

"H-hoowww diiiddd yoouuu knooww?" he asked.

"I found the contract in your desk," replied Neil.

The demon sighed and then he slowly shrank back into the form of the headmaster once more. The headmaster was nearly completely transparent, but he managed one final statement:

"Watch your back, I will return!" before completely disappearing.

Charlie looked at Neil. Neil looked at Charlie.

"Come on," said Neil, pulling Charlie up, "Let's find Kate and go home."

Chapter 15

Charlie awoke to feel the warm, autumn sun bursting through his window from outside. Charlie smiled and turned over with his eyes still shut. He lay there for a few minutes, half awake, half asleep. Suddenly he opened his eyes and the whole previous evening flashed back to him.

They had found Kate in the classroom where they had left her. Apart from a few bruises she was okay and was about to find her brothers when Charlie and Neil went in. The remaining hooded figures, whom Charlie could only assume were senior teachers, were all gone, as was the pillar of sparking light. As the teenagers looked down at the pentagram, it too faded. They looked at each other.

"Are you okay?" asked Charlie, pretending he hadn't noticed.

"I'm okay Charlie - just a bit bumped and bruised, that's all."

"I'm so glad to hear."

"Charlie?" Kate said.

"Yes?"

"Have we won?"

"Yes."

"How?"

"Ask Neil."

"Neil?"

They both looked at Neil.

"I've been wanting to know that as well," Charlie told her, "But he wouldn't tell me."

"Go on Neil," Kate said, "Please."

"Okay, okay, I was going to, but I wanted to tell both of you."

"Well I'm listening," Charlie told him.

"I'm all ears," Kate said.

And so Neil told them. About how the headmaster had left him for dead. About how he had recovered moments later. About how he had looked for the headmaster's office and how he had gone inside to look inside for something which would stop him. About how he looked inside the desk drawers and in the cupboard.

Chapter 15

About how he had found an ancient wooden box. About how he looked inside and found the document. The contract. Signed in blood. The headmaster's blood.

"And what did it say?" asked Kate, sitting on the edge of her chair in eagerness.

"It said," began Neil, pulling a sheet of paper from his pocket, "Well, you read it and find out."

Charlie and Kate grabbed it and read together the words:

"I, Edward Peter Oates, hereby swear that on this day, that I will part with my ethereal spirit, to give to the Prince of Darkness, Lord of Hell. In return for this, He will pledge that I will be granted everlasting life, unless one of the following situations occur. If any of these situations occur, the Prince of Darkness, Lord of Hell will be granted the right to take my, Edward Peter Oates', soul without ever granting me everlasting life. Also, if one of the following situations occurred, my existence in the Lands of the Living will be terminated, and I, Edward Peter Oates, will no longer have existed and no mortal will ever have remembered me.

These are the situations by which the contract will be broken:

If I, Edward Peter Oates, attempt to nullify the contract after the act of signing by any means.

If I, Edward Peter Oates, attempt to prevent the transaction taking place at the set time.

If I, Edward Peter Oates, ever come into contact with the spell contained in the glass vial, carried in the same box as this contract. Should I ever come into contact with this, the previous conditions will occur, as required by the Prince of Darkness, Lord of Hell, so that this contract is as fair to him, as it is to me.

Signed: Edward P. Oates.

Signed: P. of D., L. of H."

"Wow!" exclaimed Charlie, "Well done Neil."

"You clever thing you," said Kate.

"Well," said Neil modestly, "I couldn't have done it without Charlie fending the guy off whilst I made the search, it was nothing, really."

The teenagers went home joyously and made their way in and upstairs silently. They were exhausted after their adventure and all they wanted to do was curl up and go to bed.

That night, Charlie didn't dream his normal dream, but another, related dream.

Chapter 15

He was sitting in the dining room at the window seat when someone came in through the door. Charlie looked around and saw a man in a flat cap and tweed jacket walk towards him. The man had greasy hair, sticking out at crazy angles from beneath the hat. Charlie knew who he was.

"Hello," Charlie said.

"Hello," replied the man in a well educated voice, which didn't seem to go with the man's attire. The man continued:

"I would just like to thank you for what you and your brother and your sister did. Without you, I would have had to exist forever haunting this place, but now I am free. I don't quite know what will happen next but it can't be worse than the loneliness I have suffered since I was killed by him."

"The contract said that the headmaster would never have existed," said Charlie, "What did it mean?"

"I don't know," answered the man truthfully, "But perhaps it means that I was never murdered and I will now live my life to the full."

"I hope so," Charlie said.

"But if that happens," said the man, "you may never live here."

"Sell it then," Charlie said.

"You're right of course," said the man. "Also though, you may get a new room in your kitchen. Tomorrow, if I were you, I'd take a look behind those shelves again."

"You think so?" asked Charlie.

"Yes, I do," replied the man, before suddenly saying: "My word, what's happening?"

He was beginning to go transparent, like the headmaster did, and then he was gone, but not before he could say in an increasingly fading: "Thank you Charlie, thank you so much. I'll try not the forget you three."

"What's your name?" asked Charlie suddenly, "We never found out what your name was!"

"Robert, Robert Eves."

And then he was gone.

*   *   *

Eighty-five years previously:

Robert awoke with a start. What a horrible dream - but with a happy ending. He would have to write it down, it would make a great story. He sat up from his place at the window seat and looked outside. Up the path walked the postman, carrying just one letter.

Robert went to the door, greeted the postman and took the letter. Then he went inside to the kitchen and sat down at the kitchen table and opened the letter with a knife. Inside was some paper headed with the school emblem. It read:

"Congratulations on your promotion to the post of headmaster Mr Eves, a job which I am sure you would be well equipped to do. You have a salary increase of—"

Robert sat back in his chair with a triumphant grin on his face. So he had got the job instead of Mr Oates.

Hang on, he thought, Mr Oates? Who was Mr Oates?

*　　　　*　　　　*

Eighty-five years in the future:

Charlie got up feeling great. In fact, he thought, he had never felt better. He went into Neil's room to wake him up for school, then he went into Kate's room to wake her up. They went downstairs to the kitchen in their dressing gowns and sat down at the kitchen table.

"I can't believe last night really happened," said Charlie.

"Nor me," said Neil.

"I had another dream though," Charlie continued. Neil groaned:

"So it's not over then?" he asked.

"Oh, it's over alright, but the teacher - Robert Eves was his name - thanked us for what we did."

Kate sighed and asked:

"So what happened?"

"I'll tell you all about it." said Charlie.

And he did.